BKM Cen YP

SANTA CRUZ CITY-COUNTY LIBRARY SYSTEM

0000110968815

P9-CIT-880

DISCARDED

J 398.2 LEV
Levine, Arthur A.
The boy who drew cats /

ACA-7866

7/98

SANTA CRUZ PUBLIC LIBRARY
SANTA CRUZ, CALIFORNIA 95060

© THE BAKER & TAYLOR CO.

昔

The Boy
Who
Drew Cats

A Japanese Folktale

RETOLD BY *Arthur A. Levine*

PAINTINGS BY *Frédéric Clément*

Dial Books ⸱ *New York*

SANTA CRUZ PUBLIC LIBRARY
Santa Cruz, California

There was a time, long ago, when no winds blew, no rain fell, and the fields of Japan became parched and cracked. In this time lived a boy named Kenji, with his mother and four older brothers. They all worked hard in the fields each day, but there was not enough to eat. Small Kenji was frail, and tired easily. Try as he might, he could never help for long.

"Never mind, little one," his mother Matsuko said gently. "You can draw us some of your beautiful pictures instead." They all knew how much Kenji loved to draw.

So every day he drew cats and birds and bamboo stalks. He drew flowers that bloomed in the dried-out earth. He drew heaping plates of rice.

His brothers watched him draw at the edge of the field. "Make us something gold, Kenji!" they called.

Matsuko's worry mounted. On the farm, she feared, her youngest son would never eat well and grow strong. So she swallowed her sorrow, wrapped up Kenji's things, and took him to the village monastery.

At the dark wooden gate they were met by two priests. One was old and solemn with a beard that hung like an icicle from his chin. The other was younger and quiet too, but light danced merrily in his eyes.

"Please, sirs," Matsuko pleaded, "won't you take my youngest son for an acolyte? He will be respectful, and learn his lessons well."

"Do you wish to be a priest?" the older man asked. And the words fell like sleet on the young boy's ears.

"I wish not to be a burden," Kenji said, looking down. The older priest frowned, but the younger one whispered in his ear.

At last he nodded.

"Come," said the younger priest kindly, "my name is Takada." And together they entered the monastery, leaving Matsuko alone on the step.

Kenji struggled to please the priests. Yet the scrolls he copied grew whiskers and wings. And his mind never stayed in the gardens he was supposed to tend.

Instead he would sit near a stream of white pebbles and sketch as he always had. Takada loved Kenji's drawings, especially the ones of cats, so whenever he could, Kenji drew a cat for Takada.

But the older priest, Yoshida, remained stern as stone. It seemed that whenever Kenji stopped work for a moment and picked up his paper, Yoshida appeared overhead like a thundercloud, staring coldly.

One rainy day as Kenji swept the courtyard, he had an idea for a present to give Takada. Quickly he drew a lovely Siamese cat dancing in the rain. A few more strokes gave the cat a partner, and soon the whole page was filled with splashing, frolicking cats. Suddenly a shadow crossed the page.

"Deceitful boy!" Yoshida hissed. "I have no place in my temple for laziness. Be gone by morning." Kenji knew not to argue.

Takada appeared as Kenji was leaving. They looked at each other sadly. "Farewell, Kenji," Takada said. "You were meant to be an artist, not a priest." Then, from behind his back he brought out a delicate paper box tied in the cloth Kenji's mother had sent with him. Kenji gently untied the knot. The box contained the most beautiful set of brushes and inks he had ever seen. Kenji knew he would cry if he said so much as thank you.

"Go now," said Takada, "but remember this: AVOID LARGE PLACES AT NIGHT — KEEP TO SMALL."

Kenji wanted to ask what this meant, but he was still too close to tears. So he chanted the warning over and over to himself, down the winding path from the monastery, "Avoid large places at night. Keep to small," puzzling over its meaning.

Kenji was too ashamed to return to his family's farm. Instead he headed in the opposite direction, hoping to find another temple where he could try again to be an acolyte.

But in the next village he came to, the people were strange. When Kenji asked directions, they grew pale and stared at him, or they quickly pointed the way and scurried on.

Now it happened that there was a large and wealthy temple high at the top of a nearby mountain, where for months not a soul had entered or left. Villagers whispered that a terrible Goblin Rat, possessed of a magical sword and a fearsome tail, had claimed the temple as his own.

Kenji, however, knew none of this when he discovered the long staircase winding steeply up the mountain.

He climbed thousands of steps and reached a great gate. Then he caught his breath with a gasp of terror. On the gate, in the faintest of marks, someone had painted the Goblin Rat with his sword raised and the words "AVOID LARGE PLACES AT NIGHT. KEEP TO SM...." Whoever had begun the message had not been able to finish.

Kenji looked back, but the sun had nearly set, and he knew he couldn't risk climbing down in the dark. So he turned toward the temple, shaking.

His steps crumbled ash-white leaves at the threshold. They filled the air with dust as he pushed the door open, then settled into an awful stillness. Not a breeze stirred the stench of decay in the air.

At the end of a hallway Kenji saw a candle glowing and he crept toward it on the balls of his feet. When he had almost reached the light, Kenji thought he heard scratching behind him and he hurried into an open room.

There he found a large hall filled with white screens. They stood in a row like servants, waiting for the priests to file in for prayer. Kenji felt a little better. Maybe someone would return if he just waited a while.

Up and back Kenji paced in front of the tall white screens. Suddenly he remembered Takada's gift. He could decorate the screens while he waited! Then when the priests returned, they would see that he was worthwhile. Kenji began to paint, and what came was truly magical. In honor of Takada he painted cats. Powerful cats with broad, majestic shoulders. Sleek cats with sharp claws and quivering whiskers. Alert cats with twitching tails and watchful eyes. By the time he was done, every screen was filled and Kenji was exhausted.

Sleep pressed against his eyes, but fear kept them open. The priests had not returned, and now he heard the scratching noise again. Takada's warning came back to him with a shiver: AVOID LARGE PLACES AT NIGHT — KEEP TO SMALL. Kenji spied a small cabinet and squeezed inside. He slid the door shut and slowly, slowly his eyes began to close.

Suddenly a horrible growling and screaming woke Kenji. He heard the clash of claw and metal. The floor rumbled and a piece of the cabinet splintered off, but Kenji was too terrified to move.

At sunrise the temple was quiet again. Yet something had changed. It was the breeze! Even before he slid the door open, Kenji could feel a fresh wind sweeping through the rooms, and he could hear the cry of a crane. Still, he was unprepared for the sight that met his eyes when he finally stepped out.

The room was covered with shattered screens. Bits of wood and paper littered the floor. And as Kenji looked closer, he saw that the broken screens were empty and white. Where had all his cats gone? Kenji heard a thump and spun around. In front of him stood the one screen still intact. On it sat the King of Cats, tall and proud, with the sword of the Goblin Rat at his feet.

Kenji ran to tell the villagers the news, but they were already climbing the steps to the temple. "We felt the breeze! We heard the cranes!" they shouted. "The Goblin Rat must be dead!"

The villagers were so grateful that they invited Kenji to live and paint at the newly reopened temple. There he worked in peace and happiness, becoming a great and famous artist.

And his specialty was cats.

0000110968815

For my father, Milton L. Levine, an artist in his own right
A.A.L.
I dedicate these paintings to Hokusai
F.C.

Special thanks to Yumiko and Harry Hill, Alice North, Atsumi Sakato, Yasuko Shimizu,
Shinko and John Wheeler, and Dr. Kazuhiko Yoshimura, for their assistance.

According to Japanese legend, the famed fifteenth-century artist Sesshū Tōyō created ink drawings of animals that were so vivid, they could come alive. The tale was paraphrased into English by author Lafcadio Hearn (known in Japan, his adopted culture, as Koizumi Yakumo), whose version of *The Boy Who Drew Cats* (1898) was first printed in Tokyo by Takejiro Hasegawa as an illustrated pamphlet in the "Japanese Fairy Tale Series."

Character	Pronunciation	Meaning	Character	Pronunciation	Meaning
昔	[mukashi]	long ago...	猫	[neko]	cat
童	[warabe]	child	戦	[tatakai]	fight
願	[negai]	request, wish	閑	[kan]	quietness, calm
画	[ga]	picture, drawing	勝	[kachi]	victory
別	[wakare]	farewell, parting	福	[fuku]	happiness
霊	[rei]	goblin, spirit	完	[kan]	end
門	[mon]	gate			

Published by Dial Books / A Division of Penguin Books USA Inc.
375 Hudson Street / New York, New York 10014

Text copyright © 1993 by Arthur A. Levine / Paintings copyright © 1993 by l'école des loisirs, Paris
Design concept by Frédéric Clément / Typography by Amelia Lau Carling / Calligraphy by Sonoko Hashimoto
Printed in the U.S.A. / All rights reserved / First Edition
3 5 7 9 10 8 6 4 2

Library of Congress Cataloging in Publication Data
Levine, Arthur A., 1962–   The boy who drew cats
retold by Arthur A. Levine ; paintings by Frédéric Clément. / p. cm.
Summary: An artistic young boy's love for drawing cats gets him into trouble
and leads him to a mysterious experience. Based on a Japanese legend.
ISBN 0-8037-1172-7 (tr.). — ISBN 0-8037-1173-5 (lib)
[1. Folklore — Japan. 2. Cats — Folklore.] I. Clément, Frédéric, ill. II. Title.
PZ8.1.L437Bo   1993   398.21'0952 — dc20   91-46232   CIP   AC

The art for each painting was done in acrylics, then color-separated and reproduced in
blue, red, yellow, and black halftones. The calligraphy for the Japanese characters was done
with brush and black ink on rice paper.